ROCKEY THE OWL'S LONG JOURNEY

By Jessiey James

Illustrations by Carolyn Mottern

To order additional copies of this book, contact:
Xlibris
844-714-8691
www.Xlibris.com
Orders@Xlibris.com

ISBN:
978-1-6698-7116-3 (sc)
978-1-6698-7117-0 (hc)
978-1-6698-7115-6 (e)
Print information available on the last page

Rev. date: 03/24/2023

PREFACE

This fictional story is a story about an owl's journey. It is based upon some of the events about a northern saw-whet owl found stuck in a tree. The tree was being placed at the Rockefeller Center in New York City for the Annual Tree Lighting Ceremony. The sensational story made National News during 2020.

Rockey, an owl, was engaged in a game of Crocodile Tag with some cousins. Rockey asked another owl, George: "Crocodile, crocodile may I cross the river?" George replied: "Yes, you may, yes, you may; if you have a twig in your right claw."

Rockey had a twig in its right claw. Rockey flew across the finish line and luckily avoided being tagged by George. The owls were playing in the snow.

In the evening, Rockey flew to a nest in a tree next to a large gray farmhouse. The tree was a 75' Pine Tree. It was in Onetwo, New York.

Rockey was fast asleep in a few minutes.
Rockey was a very sound sleeper according
to its mom, Annie.

Rockey must be a very sound sleeper because while sleeping, some men from the Green Meadows Tree Company cut down the tree it was in. Rockey slept through this.

The Green Meadows Tree Company tied ropes around the large tree. They loaded the tree with Rockey in it onto a very long trailer. The trailer was hooked up to a bright blue truck.

Green Meadows Tree Company drove away with the tree and Rockey. The noise startled Rockey's family and cousins, who were sleeping in nearby trees.

Green Meadows Tree Company drove to another city
several hours away. The tree with ropes tied around it
was unloaded.

The city was getting ready for the holidays. Each
year, they would have a huge tree hauled in. The tree
was going to be put on display at the Town Square.
The city held an annual tree lighting ceremony.

That evening, Rockey's family in Onetwo, New York, discovered the tree Rockey lived in was missing. They were all wondering where Rockey had gone.

Too Too Too

Rockey woke up. It was stuck. It could not move. Immediately it yelled: "Too Too Too."

One worker, Arnie, was untying some of the ropes wrapped around the tree when he discovered Rockey. Rockey stood perfectly still and was afraid to make a sound. It thought the man staring did not look like any of the family.

Back in Onetwo, the family was looking everywhere for Rockey. Owls were swarming the area going around and around.

A woman from the Trio Wildlife Center came and picked up Rockey in the city. She placed it in a cardboard box. She wrapped an orange scarf around its neck.

After Rockey was rescued, a crane pulled the tree up onto a platform. The tree was a wreck. Several of the branches on the bottom of the tree got cut off or fell off during the ride on the long trailer.

The public complained about how bad the tree looked. It was missing so many branches. People were wondering how they were going to get it to look like a decorated tree.

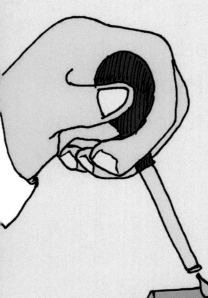

At the Trio Wildlife Center, Rockey was examined. They discovered it to be very dehydrated, cold, and had not eaten for several days. They thought Rockey was a boy owl. They began giving him drops of water with an eye dropper.

TRio WiLDLife Center

Rockey thought about his cousins and his family. Rockey wondered: "Will I miss going on the annual trip to Florida?"

Back in the city, a group began working on the tree.
They plugged branches into the tree where several
were missing. The tree was getting tree extensions.

At the Trio Wildlife Center, the people that had been taking care of Rockey got him to eat. His choice of food was mice.

Rockey's family in Onetwo were worried. They were getting ready to go to Florida. They decided to wait a few more days to see if Rockey came back. They wanted Rockey to be able to fly down with them.

HOLIDAY TREE

PROS.

- Beautiful
- smells good
- helps to celebrate the Holiday

CONS

- cost
- Was an owl's home
- What to do with the owl?

After people from the city learned that Rockey was stuck in the tree, they began questioning whether or not it was a good idea to cut the tree down and haul it to the city. After all, this uprooted an owl's home.

22

After a few days at the Trio Wildlife Center, Rockey was eating well. Then, they discovered Rockey was a girl.

Rockey was homesick. She missed playing with her cousins, especially George. She did not have anyone to play with at the Trio Wildlife Center. The only contact she had was with humans.

The Vet's Office had cleared Rockey. She was now being taken to get released at the Four Corners Preserve. She rode in a cat carrier in a white van. The van had large windows on the sides. Rockey could see some shapes.

On the way, the van drove by the tree at the Town Square. Workers started putting lights on the tree.

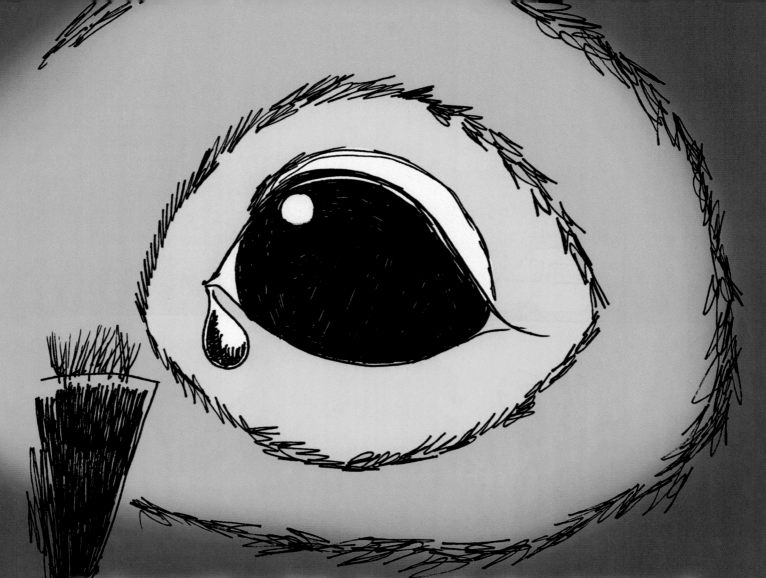

Rockey could smell the tree and make out some of the tree, her old home, now filled with bright lights. A tear ran down her eye. This was another long ride. The ride was about two hours.

The van stopped in Sugar, New York. They were at the Four Corners Preserve. They let Rockey out. Immediately, she flew to a log. Some of the people waited.

Although Rockey could not see the people, she sensed them staring at her. She flew up into a tree. This was the last time they would see her.

After Rockey flew up in the tree, immediately she met another owl, Freddie. They made plans to fly to Florida. Rockey's journey was over. She was looking forward to playing tag and seeing her family again.

Printed in the United States
by Baker & Taylor Publisher Services